Peppa Pig™

Peppa Loves School

Bath • New York • Cologne • Melbourne • Delhi
Hong Kong • Shenzhen • Singapore

Ready for School

Find and circle the Peppa who is ready for the first day of school.

Answer on page 46

Tower of Numbers

Write the correct number in the top block.

Answer on page 46

Show-and-Tell Favorites

Draw a line to match each toy that Peppa, George, and Zoe are bringing to show-and-tell to its name.

Mr. Dinosaur

Answers on page 4

Roll Call

Draw a line to match each student to what they say when Madame Gazelle takes attendance.

Answers on page 46

Rummage Sale

Peppa and her family can't wait to shop at the school's rummage sale. Find and circle three things that are different in the second picture.

Answers on page 46

Peppa's Class

Peppa's class is standing in three groups.

How many students are in Peppa's group, including Peppa?

How many students are standing with Madame Gazelle?

How many students are standing under the clock?

Answers on page 46

Art Class

In art class, Peppa decides to use the yellow paint.
Find and circle a yellow object for her to draw.

Answer on page 46

Crunching the Numbers

Rebecca Rabbit counts best when she's counting carrots. Can you do carrot math, too? Count the carrots in each row and write the total number in the circle.

=

=

=

=

Answers on page 46

On the School Playground

Draw a line from each sentence to the correct character.

Answers on page 46

What's for Breakfast?

Every school day starts with a good breakfast. Draw what Peppa is having today.

Counting Birds

Peppa loves to count birds. Count the number of birds in each picture and write the number in the space next to it.

Answers on page 46

Hide-and-Seek

Peppa and her class are playing hide-and-seek. Two of the students are hiding really well in the second picture. Put a check mark where each one was last seen.

Answers on page 46

A Special Lesson

Madame Gazelle teaches Peppa's class so many things, including how to jump in muddy puddles! Draw a line from each of these sentences to the right character.

I have a yellow raincoat and green boots.

I have yellow boots and a red coat.

I have orange boots and a purple coat.

Answers on page 46

Fun Runs

Peppa, Candy, and Suzy love to run during recess. Can you use your finger and trace along the middle of each path without touching the sides?

Finish

Finish

Finish

Alphabet Windows

Can you fill in the missing letters of the alphabet in the windows of the school?

Answers on page 46

Dance Class

Everyone loves dance class.

Find and circle the two dancers whose right leg is higher than their left.

Find and put a star next to the two dancers who have both feet on the ground.

Find and put a check mark next to the two dancers wearing tutus and jumping.

Answers on page 47

Snow Day

Peppa and George are making the most of a snowy day off from school. Draw a line from each sentence to the correct character.

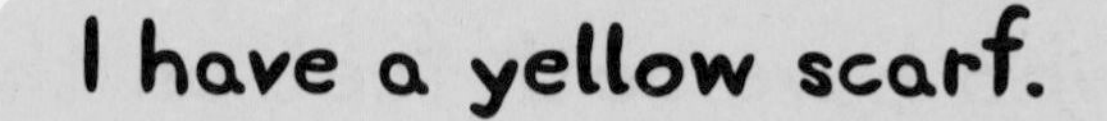

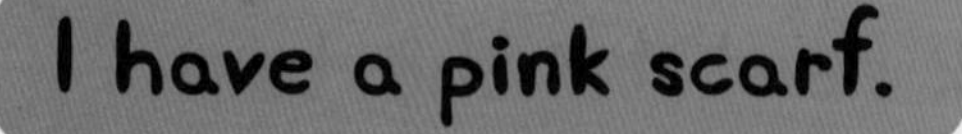

I have a green scarf.

Answers on page 47

Off to School

Zoe is in a hurry to join her friends at school. Help her get there so she can join in the fun!

Finish

Start

Answer on page 47

Who Is Taller?

For homework, Peppa and George need to see how tall they are. Draw a line to match them each with their height marks.

_______________ is taller.

Answers on page 47

Everyone's a Winner

Madame Gazelle awards her students for their hard work. They want her to have a "Best Teacher" trophy. Can you draw one for her?

Peppa with a P

Peppa's name begins with the letter P. How many things can you draw that begin with a P?

Your Name Starts with...

Circle the first letter of your name.

A B C D E F

G H I J K L

M N O P Q

R S T U V W

X Y Z

The School Play

Everyone has a part in the school play.

Find and circle the actors who play these parts:

Little Red Riding Hood

The Nurse

The Wolf

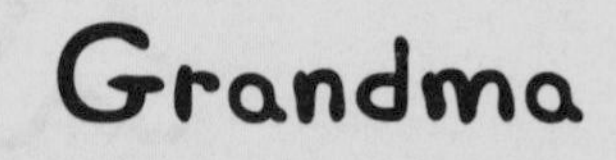

Answers on page 47

Gardeners at Work

These pictures of Peppa and George planting their own little garden at school are mixed up. Can you number them so they are in the right order?

Answer on page 47

Class Pet

It's Suzy and Peppa's turn to take care of the class pet. Draw an animal you think might be a good class pet.

Letter Match

Draw a line to match each of the uppercase letters in the window on the left with their lowercase letters in the window on the right.

Answers on page 47

Take a Look Around

Everyone in Madame Gazelle's class is looking around for something to paint. Can you see where each close-up belongs in the bigger picture? Draw a line to each one that you can find.

Answers on page 47

School Books

Find and circle these favorite books for story time.

Candy's favorite book is about a tiger.

Gerald likes to hear stories about giraffes.

Peppa loves any book with lots of letters and words in it.

Answers on page 47

Lunch Time!

Oh no! George forgot his lunch box. Can you find him a sandwich, some fruit, and a drink?

Answers on page 4

Play with Clay

Everyone stretches their imagination with clay.

Put a star next to the pink dinosaur.

Add a check mark next to the teapot with the blue handle.

Draw a circle around the yellow tree.

Answers on page 47

A Musical Family

Peppa and George learned how to play instruments in school and can now play with Mummy and Daddy Pig. Match each instrument to its name.

Horn

Violin

Accordion

Drum

Answers on page 47

Class Trip

George's favorite part of a class trip to the museum is the dinosaur room!

Put a check mark next to the bony dinosaur with the open mouth.

Draw a circle around the animal with wings.

Put a star next to the dinosaur with spots on its back and tail.

Answers on page 47

Miss Rabbit's Bus!

Get Miss Rabbit to the school bus so she can pick up the students at the end of the school day.

Answer on page 47

Rock Collection

Peppa's class is collecting all the interesting rocks they find.

Put a circle around the gray rocks.

Draw an X next to the purple rocks.

Put a check mark next to the yellow rock.

nswers on page 48

Happy School Friends

Put a check mark next to the row of school friends that is not like the others.

Answer on page 4

All-Together Fun

Trace over the dotted line to make a jump rope long enough for Peppa and all her school friends to jump over.

Arts and Crafts

Which four things are missing from the table in the second picture?

Answers on page 48

Swimming Lessons

Can you help Richard Rabbit paddle over to George so they can take their swimming lesson together?

Answer on page 48

Camping Out

Peppa is all ready for her school camping trip. Circle the animals she is likely to see in the woods.

Answers on page 4

Practice Makes Perfect

Trace over the shapes on this page so maybe one day you can paint them as nicely as George made this circle.

Snack Time

Draw the small hand pointing to the 2 and the big hand pointing to the 12 on the clock. Then circle the number in the window that tells you what time it is.

Answers on page 4

The School Race

Emily Elephant wins the school race! Draw a line between each racer and the color of his or her baton.

Answers on page 48

Bath Time

Part of getting ready for the next day of school includes taking a nice warm bath every night. Draw a line between these close-ups and where they go in the bigger picture.

Answers on page 48

Holiday Party

Today's the school Halloween party!

Find and circle the table that has three glowing pumpkins on it.

Find and circle two spider balloons.

Find and circle the student holding a pumpkin.

Find and circle two bats.

Answers on page 48

Answers

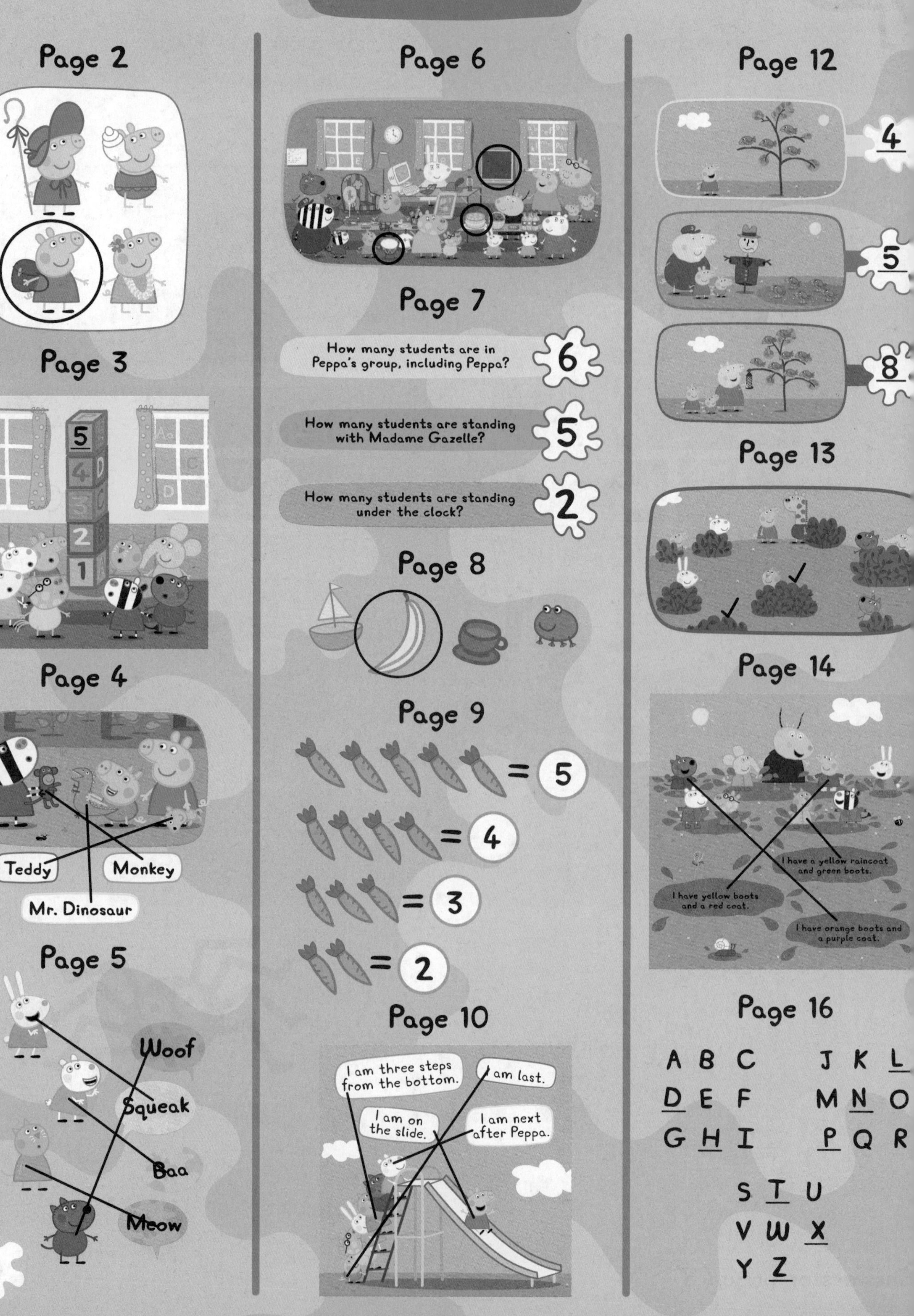
Page 2
Page 3
5
4
3
2
1
Page 4
Teddy
Monkey
Mr. Dinosaur
Page 5
Woof
Squeak
Baa
Meow
Page 6
Page 7
How many students are in Peppa's group, including Peppa?
6
How many students are standing with Madame Gazelle?
5
How many students are standing under the clock?
2
Page 8
Page 9
= 5
= 4
= 3
= 2
Page 10
I am three steps from the bottom.
I am last.
I am on the slide.
I am next after Peppa.
Page 12
4
5
8
Page 13
Page 14
I have a yellow raincoat and green boots.
I have yellow boots and a red coat.
I have orange boots and a purple coat.
Page 16
A B C
D E F
G H I
J K L
M N O
P Q R
S T U
V W X
Y Z

Answers

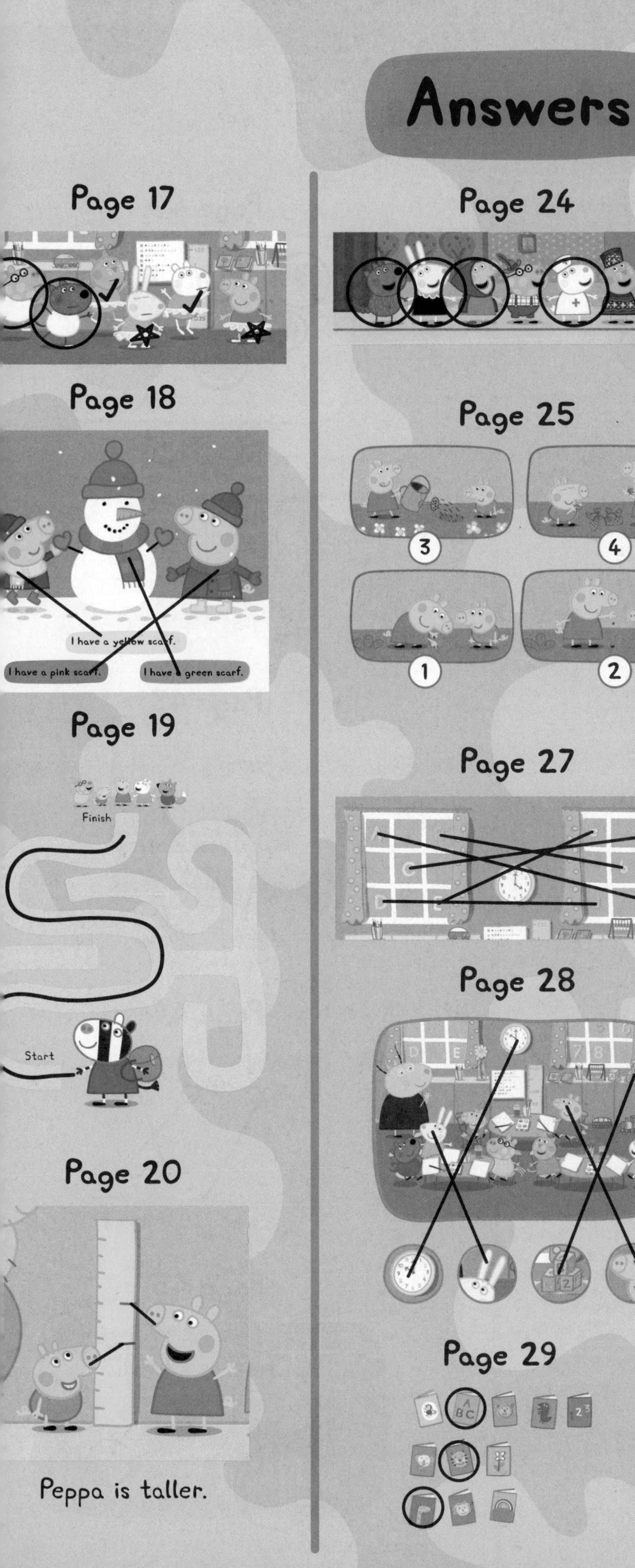

Peppa is taller.

Answers

Page 35

Page 36

Page 38

Page 39

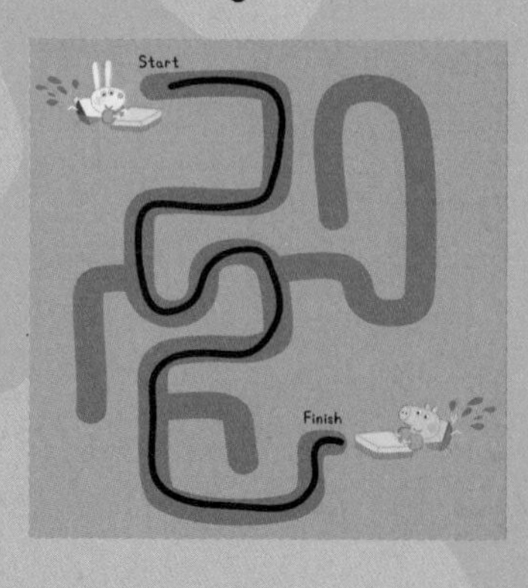

Page 40

Page 42

Page 43

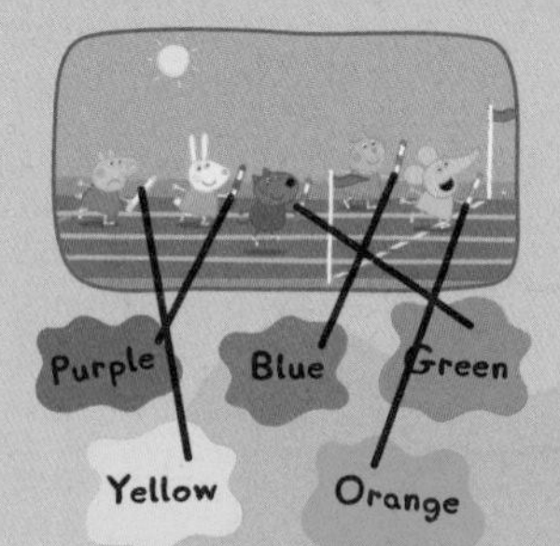

Page 44

Page 45